Fanny

Written by Stephen Cosgrove
Illustrated by Robin James

A Serendipity™ Book

PSS!
PRICE STERN SLOAN

The Serendipity™ series was created by Stephen Cosgrove and Robin James

Copyright © 2002, 1986 by Price Stern Sloan. All rights reserved.
Published by Price Stern Sloan, a division of Penguin Putnam Books for Young Readers,
345 Hudson Street, New York, New York 10014

ISBN 0-8431-4888-8

Revised Edition: 2002 printing

Dedicated to the dearest of the dear,
Susan Malarky and Patti Kelly.
They showed me that being handicapped
is a state of mind.

— Stephen

Beyond the horizon, farther than far, in the middle of the Crystal Sea, is a beautiful island called Serendipity. On the south side of the island was an old wooden fence. The fence stretched for miles and miles with only sweet smelling lilac and an occasional honeysuckle rose for companions.

At the very end of the fence was a lovely old farm nestled at the top of a wooded hill. The farm was filled with all sorts of animals: chickens, cows, and sheep.

Amidst the animals of this old barnyard lived a fluffy, grey cat named Fanny. In many ways Fanny was an ordinary cat. She had an ordinary long, swishy tail like all the other cats. She had ordinary green eyes that looked at all the world in wonder like all the other cats. Ordinary, yes, but different too, for Fanny had just three legs.

Because Fanny had only three legs instead of four she had to hobble and hop to and fro to get to there and back again. She hopped to get a drink of milk and afterwards she hopped atop the fence to sun herself on a warm spring day.

Although she had but three legs she got around pretty well. In fact, she needed no help from any of the other animals in the barnyard.

Oddly, the other farm animals never talked to Fanny because they felt it was kind of embarrassing to talk to a creature who was handicapped.

Whenever Fanny hobbled by, the chickens would turn their backs, ruffle their feathers, and look the other way. Sometimes a chick would try to talk to her but one of the old hens would always come kickling and cackling and shoo the chick away. "Don't talk to her little chick-chick. It would do nothing more than embarrass her. Besides she has nothing to say."

Fanny would act as if she hadn't heard and hobble on her way.

Whenever she hopped by the barn all of the cows would gawk and stare with big, brown eyes as she passed. If one of the calves tried to stick its neck through the fence to talk to her, one of the old, bossy milk cows would moo it away and say, "Don't stare, you silly calf. You'll just embarrass her. Besides she has nothing to say."

Fanny would just pretend she didn't hear as she batted at a bumble bee or a butterfly that happened to be flying by.

When Fanny hobbled the well-worn path in the pasture, the little spring lambs would gather to talk to her as she limped by. No sooner would they start rushing through the clover than an old ewe would call them back to the herd. "Come back little lambs and don't be bad! You'll just embarrass her. Besides she has nothing to say."

Poor Fanny would just continue on her way.

There also lived on the farm an orphaned little Jack Russell puppy named Ruby. Ruby had no parents that anyone could remember, and slept alone in an old building filled with hay.

Ruby loved everybody and everything. Best of all she loved to kiss and lick the other animals of the farm. It was the same: kisses and licks, kisses and licks. Ruby was the fastest licker around.

With tail wagging she would sidle up to a baby chicken and before that chick could let out a kickle or a cackle Ruby's tongue was out, the lick was licked.

Well, all the animals had been licked and loved by Ruby so much that one day an old ewe and a cow cruelly dared the little puppy to kiss old Fanny as she hobbled on her way.

Ruby took the dare, and hiding in the tall clover that grew by the fence, she waited for the cat to come by.

Sure enough, in no time at all old Fanny came hobbling along. With a giggle, Ruby dashed from the clover and gave Fanny a long and loving slurp from the tip of her nose to the top her head.

That little dog surely was the fastest licker around.

Old Fanny didn't complain. She didn't say, "Yuck" nor did she try to wipe the kiss away. Instead, she just licked and kissed that puppy right back, lick for lick. Contrary to what the barnyard animals had thought, Fanny wasn't embarrassed in the slightest. More importantly, she had *a lot* to say.

Ruby and Fanny sat around for the longest time licking, and loving, and laughing, and talking about this and that.

Later, in the old wooden barn, they lay down together in a warm pile of hay, curled up in each other's love.

From that day forward the two of them were thought of as one, and together they shared all the farm had to share. Together they hobbled and walked from here to there and back again.

Together they stopped and talked to the chicks about the weather and the sunflowers that grew so very tall.

The chicks were delighted to find that Fanny wasn't embarrassed by her handicap at all and that she had a lot to say.

Together the dog and cat mooed with the calves in the dairy barn. The calves were so moved by what Fanny had to say that they shared some milk from the old bossy cow that just looked the other way.

That cat mewed and meowed happily about her life on the farm, a long cat's tale she had never been able to share before.

Together Fanny and Ruby walked through the meadow of deep purple clover talking to the lambs as they frolicked and played. And they, too, learned that this wonderful cat had a heart full of things she wanted to say.

From that day forward the lambs, the calves, the chicks, a scruffy little puppy named Ruby and a three legged cat named Fanny were the best of friends.

Fanny had never been handicapped by what she was, only by what the other animals thought she was.

IF YOU HOP, HOBBLE, OR WHEEL

FEELING YOU'RE THE HANDICAPPED KIND

REMEMBER YOU ARE JUST WHO YOU ARE

AND HANDICAP IS BUT A STATE OF MIND.

Serendipity™ Books

Created by
Stephen Cosgrove and Robin James

Enjoy all the delightful books in the Serendipity™ Series:

Available wherever books are sold.